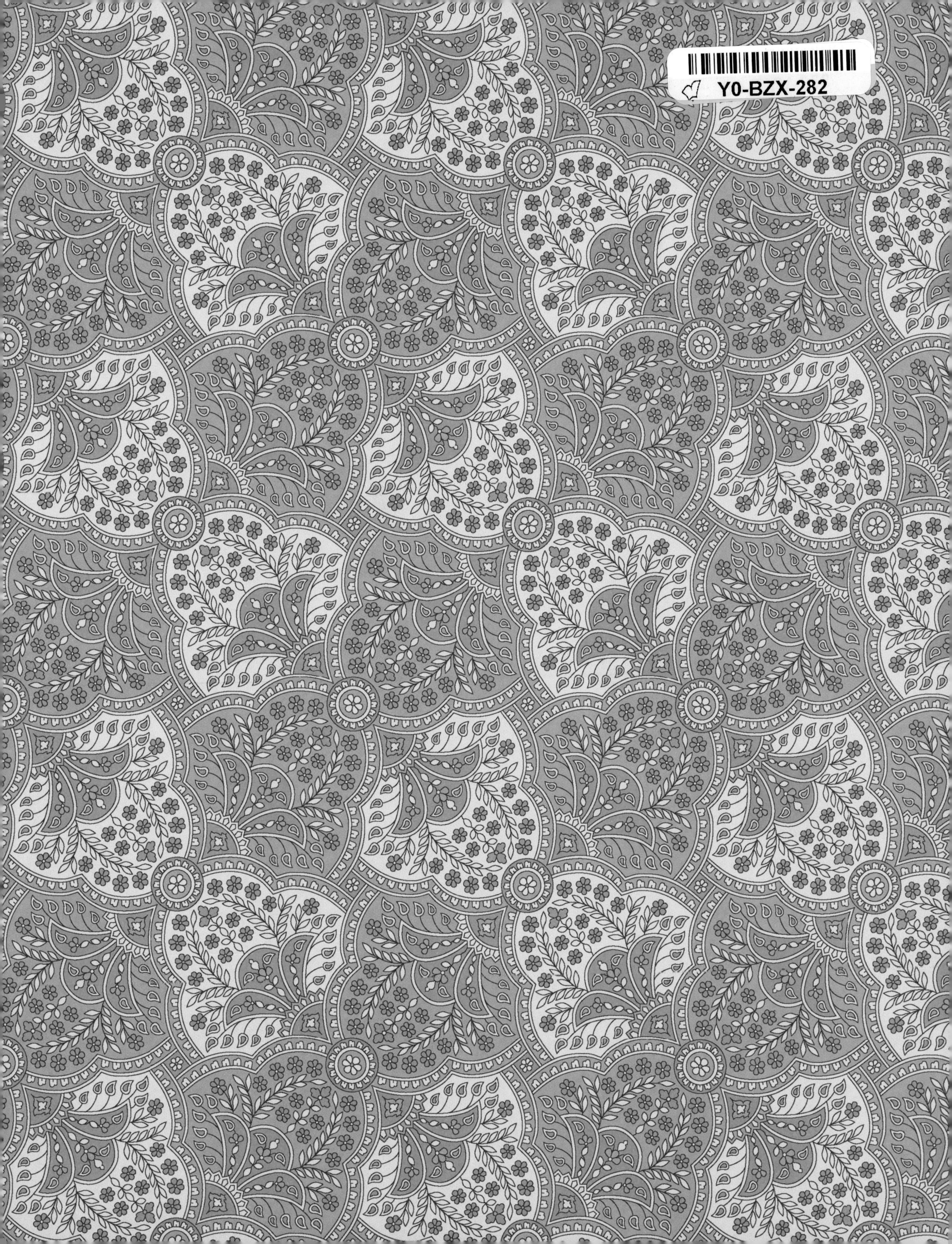
Y0-BZX-282

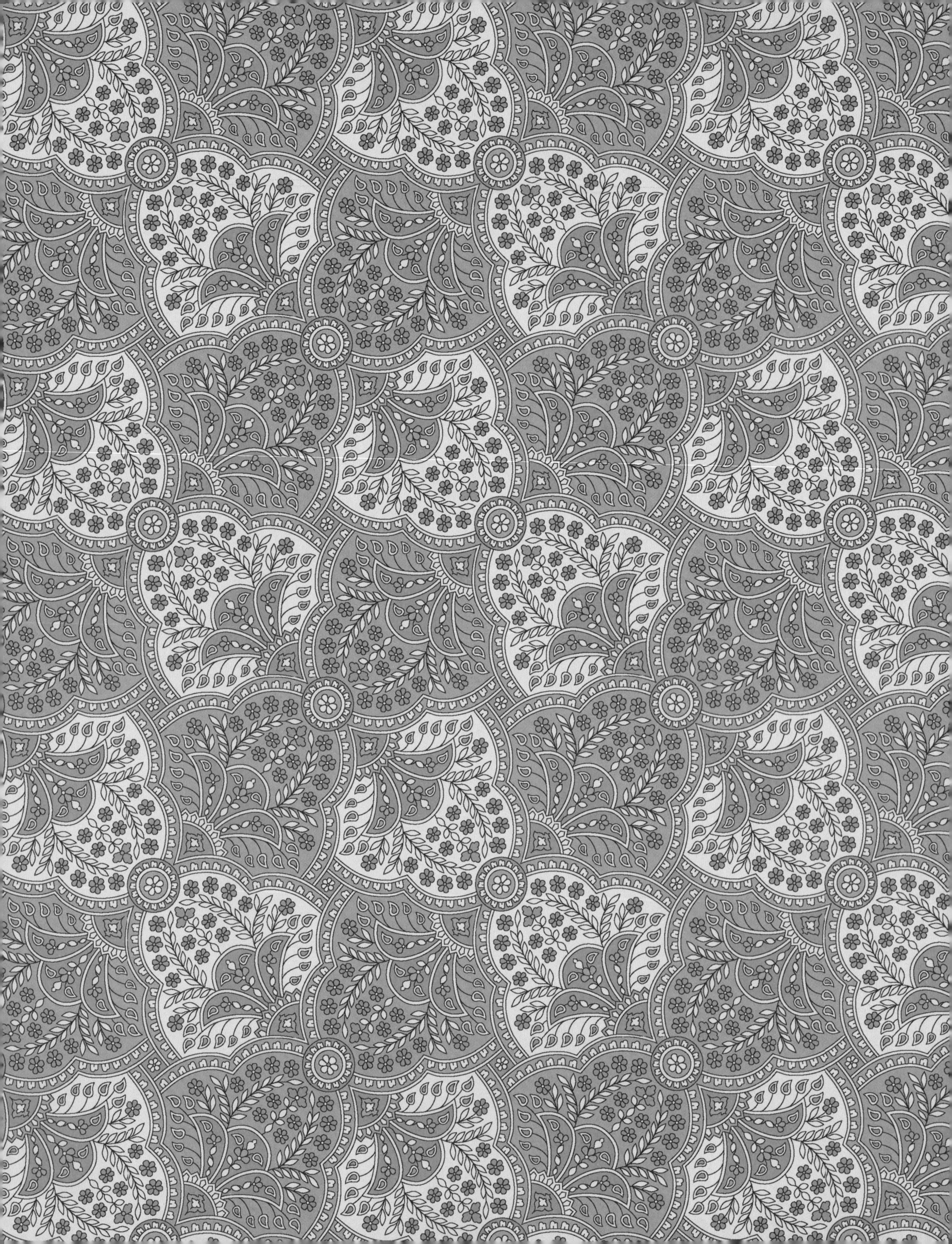

TREASURY OF

Fairy Tales

Cover illustrated by Martha Avilés

Louis Weber, C.E.O., Publications International, Ltd.
7373 North Cicero Avenue, Lincolnwood, Illinois 60712

Ground Floor, 59 Gloucester Place, London W1U 8JJ

Customer Service: 1-800-595-8484 or customer_service@pilbooks.com

www.pilbooks.com

p i kids is a trademark of Publications International, Ltd., and is registered in the United States.

8 7 6 5 4 3 2 1

Manufactured in China.

ISBN-10: 1-4508-1902-8
ISBN-13: 978-1-4508-1902-2

TREASURY OF
Fairy Tales

publications international, ltd.

Contents

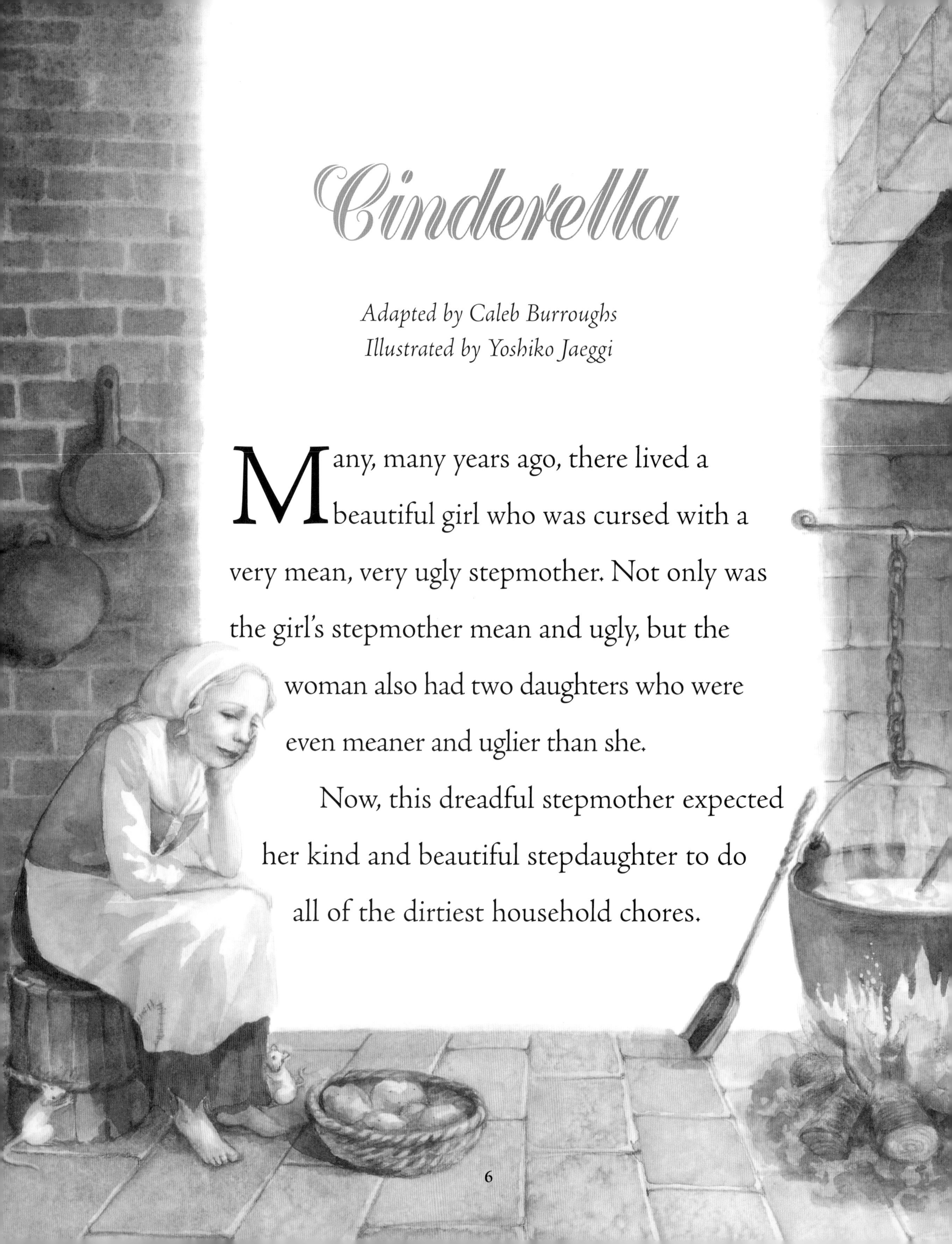

Cinderella

Adapted by Caleb Burroughs
Illustrated by Yoshiko Jaeggi

Many, many years ago, there lived a beautiful girl who was cursed with a very mean, very ugly stepmother. Not only was the girl's stepmother mean and ugly, but the woman also had two daughters who were even meaner and uglier than she.

Now, this dreadful stepmother expected her kind and beautiful stepdaughter to do all of the dirtiest household chores.

The girl peeled potatoes and scrubbed the floors. She washed the dishes and split the firewood.

But none of these tasks was as dirty as scooping the cinders and ash from the fireplace.

"Cinderella!" her stepsisters would chant. "Clean the cinders right away, Cinderella!"

"Cinderella," her stepmother would demand, "scrub the fireplace until it shines! I don't want to see a single cinder left!"

So the beautiful girl worked in dirt and ash, and the awful name clung to her. While her stepsisters wore gorgeous gowns and jewelry, the girl now known as Cinderella wore rags and scrubbed the fireplace.

One day, a messenger arrived with a very important delivery. It was an invitation to the prince's ball.

"Oooh!" squealed one of the terrible stepsisters. "I hope the handsome prince will ask me to dance with him!"

"He will surely ask me," said the other stepsister. "I am the most beautiful young lady in all the kingdom!"

"I know the prince will be enchanted by both of you," declared their mother. "You are both lucky to be blessed with my good looks — unlike our little Cinderella."

The stepsisters turned to look at Cinderella, and they giggled at her dirty clothes.

On the night of the ball, the stepsisters squeezed into their gowns and ordered Cinderella around. They cackled at her and made her do their bidding.

"Ouch! You are pulling my hair!" yelled one stepsister.

"While we are dancing with the handsome prince, Cinderella will be tidying the house," laughed the other.

Cinderella watched sadly as they left for the ball.

When she was alone, Cinderella sat down in the garden and sobbed.

"Why must I work all day and be wretched and dirty?" poor Cinderella asked herself. "If only I could go and dance at the ball, just for one night!"

Cinderella was surprised by a flash of light. Before her appeared a winged woman dressed in a flowing gown.

"Who are you?" asked a very startled Cinderella.

"Why, I'm your fairy godmother," answered the woman.

"My fairy godmother?" asked Cinderella.

"Yes," said the woman. "I am here to help you. I have watched while your family has mistreated you, and I have come to help bring you the good fortune you deserve. Tonight is the night of the royal ball, is it not?"

Cinderella wiped away a tear and nodded her head.

"Would you like to go?" asked the fairy godmother.

"More than anything!" answered Cinderella. "My stepsisters have already gone. But I must stay here, and I have nothing but tattered old rags to wear."

"Leave that to me," said the fairy godmother.

With a wave of her wand, the fairy godmother showered the garden with sparks. When Cinderella opened her eyes she was amazed by what she saw.

"Why, my rags have turned into a beautiful gown!" exclaimed Cinderella. "Look at these lovely glass slippers! The pumpkins and mice from the garden are a coach and a team of fine horses! How did you do this?"

"There is no time for questions," said the fairy godmother. "You hurry to the ball, for my magic spell will be broken once the clock strikes twelve. You must leave before midnight!"

Dressed in her splendid gown and riding in her fine horse-drawn coach, Cinderella arrived at the ball.

"Who is that stunning girl?" asked one of the guests.

"She must be royalty," said another.

When the handsome prince spotted the gorgeous young woman, he asked her to dance. Cinderella smiled with joy as she took his hand.

"Who does that girl think she is?" cried the two stepsisters. They had no idea that the stranger was really their stepsister Cinderella.

Throughout the night, the prince danced only with Cinderella. The other girls had come to the ball hoping to make the prince fall in love with them. But the prince's eyes never left Cinderella — and she never left his side.

Dancing with the prince, Cinderella felt herself falling in love.

"I have never had such a wonderful time," Cinderella told the prince.

The prince was falling in love, too.

"Who are you?" he asked Cinderella.

Before Cinderella could answer, the clock began to strike twelve. She had forgotten all about her fairy godmother's warning!

As the clock continued to chime, Cinderella rushed from the prince's arms.

"I must get home," she thought to herself. "I cannot let the prince see me in my filthy rags."

"Come back!" cried the startled prince. "You did not even tell me your name!"

But Cinderella did not hear him, for she was already through the palace doors and racing down the steps. In her hurry, she dropped one of her glass slippers.

The prince rushed after her. He did not see the beautiful girl that he loved, but he did find the little glass slipper she had left behind. As he picked up the shoe, he vowed he would see her again.

The next day, Cinderella was again dressed in rags, cleaning her stepmother's house. As she scrubbed, she heard her stepsisters talking excitedly.

"The prince is searching the country for the girl he loves, the one he danced with at the ball," said one.

"He has her glass slipper with him. He has sworn to marry the girl who fits the shoe!" said the other stepsister.

Before long, the prince arrived at the home of Cinderella's stepmother, and he was carrying her glass slipper.

Cinderella watched, hidden in a corner, as each of her selfish stepsisters tried on the slipper. But their feet were far too big for the delicate shoe. The prince was starting to leave when he spotted Cinderella.

"Won't you try on the slipper?" asked the handsome prince.

"Dirty Cinderella?" laughed the wicked stepmother. "Certainly she is not the girl you love!"

But the prince insisted. Sure enough, Cinderella's dainty foot fit perfectly inside the glass slipper. The prince had found his love at last!

Cinderella and the prince were soon married. They lived happily ever after.

Rapunzel

Adapted by Caleb Burroughs
Illustrated by Kathi Ember

There once was a powerful and dreadful witch. This witch lived in a high castle that overlooked a garden. And in this garden grew the freshest and most beautiful fruits and vegetables.

Next to the witch's land stood a sad and tiny ramshackle cottage in which lived a poor man and his wife. The wife was expecting the couple's first child.

One evening, as the couple sat eating their dinner of hard bread and cold beans, the wife had a craving.

"My dear husband," she said, "I would love just a nibble of the fresh rapunzel lettuce that grows in the witch's garden. It would taste so much better than these cold beans and stale bread."

So later that night, the poor man climbed the fence to the witch's garden and headed into the patch of rapunzel lettuce.

Just as he knelt to pick the freshest head of lettuce he could find, the man heard a wicked cackle. He spun around to see the witch!

"How dare you enter my garden!" screeched the witch. "And what do I see? You were trying to steal some of my delicious rapunzel lettuce? Why, I never!"

The man cowered among the vegetables, begging the angry witch not to hurt him. "I meant no harm. I was merely trying to pick a bit for my hungry wife," he cried. "Let me go home to her, for she is expecting our first child."

"Go home," replied the witch. "Take all that you want from my garden. But when your child comes, I shall take her for my own!"

The scared man hurried home, his pockets full of rapunzel lettuce. Soon, his wife had her fill of the fresh lettuce. She loved it so much that she decided to name her child after the delicious vegetable. Her husband did not tell her about the witch's nasty threat.

A short time later, a baby girl was born. The woman named her child Rapunzel.

Before the sun went down that day, there was a knock on the door. The man opened the door and the wicked old witch rushed into the cottage!

"As I promised," said the witch, "I am here to take your only child for my own."

"What is she talking about?" the woman asked her husband. But the poor couple could do nothing, and the witch took the baby girl from them.

Now, while this witch was very mean, she was also very smart. She knew that the child's parents might try to find her, so she locked Rapunzel in a high tower.

Days turned into months, and months turned into years, while little Rapunzel grew from an infant into a beautiful young woman.

During her many years in the tower, Rapunzel had never been allowed to cut her hair. So it had grown long — very, very long. Her two golden braids had grown so long, in fact, that the witch put them to good use. The window to Rapunzel's tower room was very high, so to reach it, the witch would call:

"Rapunzel, Rapunzel,
Throw down your gold hair!"

Rapunzel would obey, and the witch would scurry up the two golden braids.

One day, a handsome prince was traveling through the forest. From a distance, he heard a girl's voice singing a lovely song.

The prince was following the sound of the beautiful voice when suddenly he heard a scratchy, ugly voice croak:

"Rapunzel, Rapunzel,

Throw down your gold hair!"

Through his spyglass, the prince was surprised to see a beautiful girl with long golden hair. She was perched in a tower window. He spotted an ugly old witch climbing up her golden braids.

In his hiding spot in the woods, the handsome prince waited until the old witch left the tower. Enchanted by the beautiful girl and her lovely voice, the curious prince crept up to the tower.

"Rapunzel, Rapunzel, throw down your gold hair!" called the prince. Sure enough, as soon as he had finished saying these words, two golden braids fell from the high window. Taking hold of them, the prince climbed up the tower wall until he reached the beautiful girl.

"Who are you?" the prince asked.

"I am Rapunzel," she replied. "An old witch took me from my parents when I was but a baby. I have lived locked in this tower ever since."

"I will save you," said the prince.

He climbed down the tower wall to the ground below. There he stood while Rapunzel leaped from the window into his arms. A moment later, they spotted the witch returning to the tower.

The prince and Rapunzel quickly hid in the bushes. From their hiding place, they could hear the witch call out, "Rapunzel, Rapunzel, throw down your gold hair!"

This time, no braids of hair fell from the window. The witch soon realized what had happened. "Alas, Rapunzel has escaped! Now I will be all alone for the rest of my days!"

Rapunzel and the prince stayed hidden and watched as the old witch wandered off into the forest, whining and moaning and gnashing her teeth at having lost the prisoner from her tower.

Once they could no longer hear the witch, the prince helped Rapunzel onto his horse. They rode away, and they did not stop until they reached Rapunzel's village.

Just as the sun was beginning to set, the prince and Rapunzel finally arrived at the home of her parents. It had been many years since the witch had stolen their child, and the poor man and his wife had grown very old. Yet their tired faces transformed at the sight of the beautiful girl with the golden hair.

"I am your daughter, Rapunzel," said the girl.

Her parents hugged her tightly as their faces beamed with joy. They had never given up hope that they would see their daughter again someday.

"This brave and handsome prince rescued me from the old witch," continued Rapunzel. "He would like for all of us to come live in his castle."

Rapunzel's parents did not care where they lived as long as they were with their beloved daughter. They gladly packed up their belongings and moved to the prince's beautiful castle. And they all lived happily ever after.

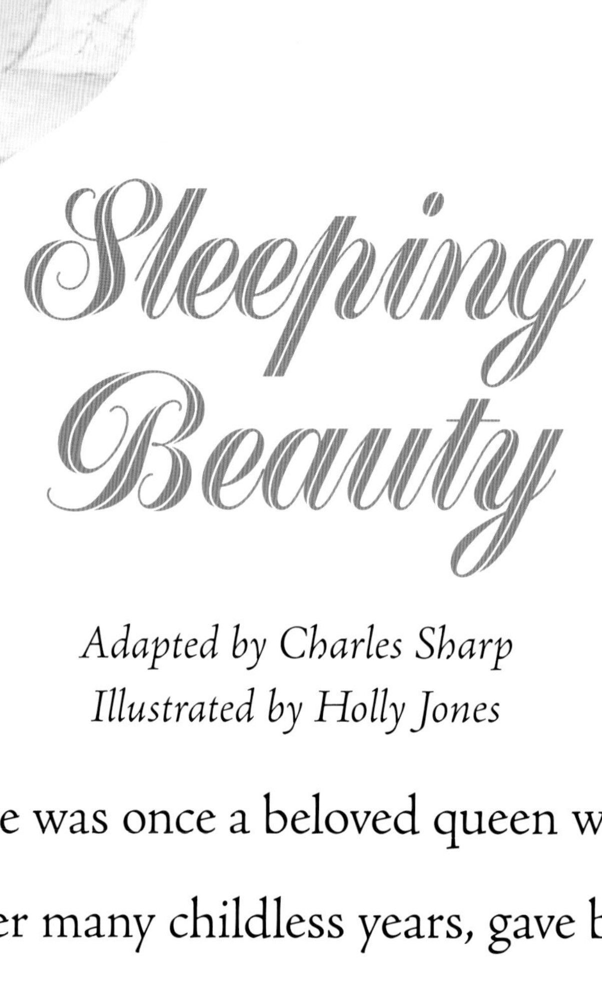

Sleeping Beauty

Adapted by Charles Sharp
Illustrated by Holly Jones

There was once a beloved queen who, after many childless years, gave birth to a beautiful daughter. The queen's loyal subjects prepared a festival to welcome the baby princess.

Deep in a dark forest of the same kingdom, there lived a wicked witch who led a lonely life. "Bah!" cried the bitter witch. "I'll put a stop to all these cheers!"

With evil in her heart, the witch set out for the castle. The moment she arrived, the cruel witch cast a terrible spell on the princess.

"On her sixteenth birthday," hissed the witch, "the princess will prick her finger and fall into a deep sleep and she will never awaken!"

The queen gasped. Holding her baby close, she whispered, "I promise to do my best to keep you away from danger."

Sixteen years later, the princess prepared for her birthday party. She noticed a tiny rip in her dress and decided to mend it herself. But as she stitched, the princess pricked her finger on the sharp needle. As the witch had predicted, the princess at once fell into a deep sleep.

The queen was horrified to find her daughter fast asleep on the floor of the sewing room. She knew at once what had happened. The princess was brought to her own room and put to bed.

The devastated queen summoned all of the best doctors, witches, and wizards to the castle, but they were unable to reverse the evil spell.

One day, a fairy arrived at the castle to see the lovely princess at rest.

The fairy sat with the girl for a long time, whispering comforting words in her ear.

"I have news about your daughter," the fairy told the queen. In her travels, the fairy had met a bitter old witch who bragged about her powerful spells. The sneering witch had mentioned the one thing that could break her formidable sleeping spell.

"True love," the fairy told the queen. "If a man of pure heart falls in love with the princess, she will awaken."

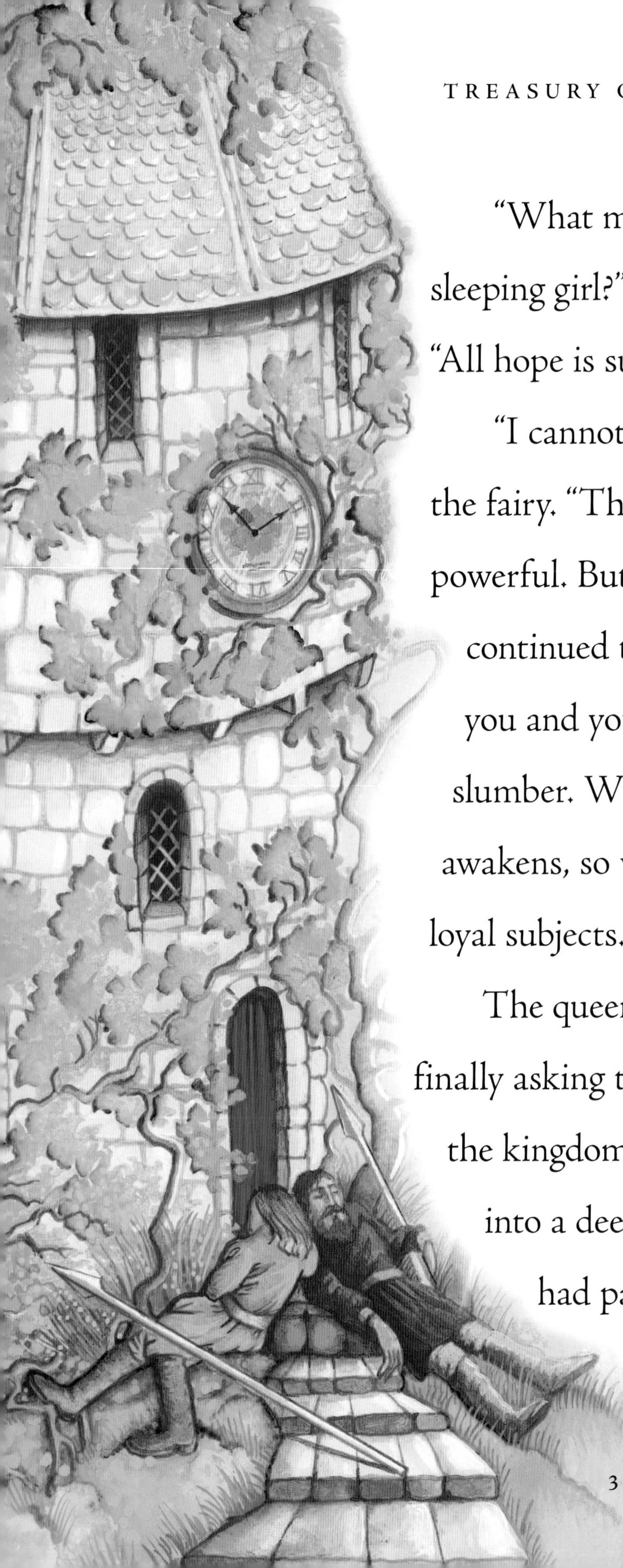

"What man would fall in love with a sleeping girl?" asked the queen, sighing. "All hope is surely lost."

"I cannot awaken your daughter," said the fairy. "The witch's magic is too powerful. But I can bring you comfort," continued the fairy. "I can cast a spell so you and your subjects share the princess's slumber. When the princess finally awakens, so will you and your legions of loyal subjects."

The queen sat deep in thought before finally asking the fairy to cast her spell on the kingdom. Soon, everyone had settled into a deep sleep. After a hundred years had passed, a forest had grown around the silent castle.

One day a young, handsome prince who was riding his horse through the thick forest glimpsed a stone wall. The prince cautiously went a bit closer.

"A hidden castle!" the prince exclaimed. He cleared away vines and found a doorway. Then he noticed a sleeping guard who would not awaken. So the prince decided to enter the castle and investigate.

The prince walked through a great hall, and he found more sleeping people with every step he took.

"Wake up!" he shouted, but it was no use. Everyone continued to sleep very soundly.

Soon the prince came to the princess's room. "She is beautiful," he whispered in awe.

The prince gazed at her peaceful face and stepped by the girl's bedside to gently kiss her hand. At the prince's kiss, the princess's eyes opened in a flash. She gazed at the young man sitting beside her.

"It's you," she said softly. "A kind fairy told me that you would come here to save me!"

At that moment, the queen and her subjects also awoke from their sleep, and the queen rushed to the princess's room.

"My daughter!" she said, overjoyed. "You have finally come back to me!"

The queen looked at the prince. He was the man of pure heart whom the fairy had described.

"Thank you," she said, embracing him. "You have saved my daughter and the entire kingdom!"

As the people rubbed the sleep of a hundred years from their eyes, the queen's joyful cries soon reached their ears. Everyone hurried to see the princess. "Our princess is awake!" they cheered, already celebrating.

The queen introduced her subjects to the prince.

"This man loves my daughter," said the queen, "and they will be married as soon as possible. We have waited a long time for this day. Let us not waste another moment!"

Her subjects all looked forward to the royal wedding, and in a few short days, the sound of wedding bells rang throughout the kingdom.

The prince and princess were married in the finest ceremony anyone had ever seen. Their subjects ate and drank and sang and danced. The prince, his heart filled with love, had never been happier. And the princess had truly found the man of her dreams. The two of them lived in a grand and beautiful castle happily ever after.

Three Golden Flowers

Adapted by Lisa Harkrader
Illustrated by Marty Noble

Once there was a chief who ruled an island tribe. He lived a happy life until one day his daughter became very ill. The chief called for the tribe's healers. The healers did everything they could for the princess; they gave her herbs, bathed her in oils, and burned spices to soothe her.

But the princess continued to grow weaker. Soon she could barely lift her head from her pillow. The chief was deeply concerned, and he sent for the tribal wise man.

"Find three golden orchids," the wise man said upon examining the princess. "Their scent will cure her."

"Where are these golden flowers?" asked the chief.

"They grow only where the sun shines through the water," said the wise man.

The chief proclaimed that any man who could bring him the three golden orchids could marry the princess.

The great warriors of the tribe, eager to earn the princess's hand in marriage, explored every inch of the island. But they could not find any golden orchids.

On a nearby island, a poor man lived with his wife and three sons. The sons were not great warriors; they were modest farmers, like their father.

When the family heard the chief's proclamation, they were excited. They knew exactly where to find the flowers that would cure the princess. Each year, nine perfect orchids — delicate and golden — grew behind a waterfall in a hidden valley.

The eldest of the brothers went to the valley and picked the three largest orchids.

He placed them carefully in a basket and set off in his canoe across the tranquil sea.

When the eldest brother reached the chief's island, he met an old fisherman on the beach.

"What have you there?" asked the fisherman.

The young man knew that everyone was searching for the orchids. He was afraid the old man would steal the basket if he knew what treasure lay inside.

"Fishing worms," the young man said.

The fisherman smiled and allowed him to continue.

The young man reached the village, and soon he stood before the chief. When he opened his basket, he was surprised to find worms, just as he had told the fisherman.

When the eldest brother returned home, the middle brother decided to try his luck. He, too, met the fisherman on the beach. Like his older brother, he was suspicious and lied to the fisherman.

Later, when he met the chief, he also found his basket filled with worms.

Now only three golden orchids remained. The youngest brother picked them and set off to see the chief.

When the boy encountered the fisherman, he was honest and said, "I carry flowers to cure the princess."

The fisherman was pleased that the boy told the truth and gave him a bamboo flute for good luck.

The boy thanked the fisherman and ran to the village. At first, the wary chief refused to see him. But the boy opened his basket to reveal the golden orchids. They were as perfect as when he had first picked them.

As soon as the princess smelled the orchids, her eyes opened. She looked up and smiled. She thanked the boy.

Soon, the two were laughing and talking together.

The chief was pleased that his daughter was cured, but he did not want her to marry a poor farmer's son.

"Now you must prove that you are worthy to marry her," said the chief. "Tomorrow, take a hundred parrots into the forest. By nightfall, you must bring them all back safely. If any are missing, you cannot marry my daughter."

The boy spent the next day chasing the parrots, but when the sun had set, he could not find a single one. Suddenly, he remembered the lucky bamboo flute. He trilled a few notes, and all of the parrots flew to him.

When the young man returned with all one hundred parrots, the chief could not believe his eyes.

"If my daughter will have you," said the chief humbly, "then I will welcome you into our family."

When they were older, the princess did indeed marry this boy. They lived happily ever after on the island.

Vasilissa and the Magic Doll

Adapted by Regina Duffin
Illustrated by Nan Brooks

Long ago in faraway Russia, there lived a merchant, his wife, and their young daughter, Vasilissa.

Sadly, Vasilissa's mother became ill.

"Beloved daughter," Vasilissa's mother said, "I am dying. But do not worry. I have made you a doll to keep with you always. You must not tell anyone about her."

Vasilissa took the doll and slipped it into her pocket.

"Whenever you are afraid or sad," said her mother, "give the doll a bit to eat and drink. Then tell her your troubles. She will let you know just what to do."

Vasilissa kissed her mother.

"Bless you, child, and do not cry," said her mother.

Her mother slowly closed her eyes and said, "I will always be here with you, my child."

Vasilissa tried not to cry. She reached for the doll and gave her a tiny piece of bread and a drop of milk. She whispered, "I am sad because I miss my mother."

Vasilissa heard a tiny voice say, "Do not cry, little Vasilissa. Go to sleep. The morning is wiser than the evening." Vasilissa curled up in her bed and fell asleep.

One day, Vasilissa's father returned home from a trip with a new wife. She had two older daughters who were jealous of Vasilissa's beauty. Vasilissa's stepmother was as cruel as Vasilissa was kind. She dealt very harshly with the sweet and gentle girl.

The stepmother and her daughters made Vasilissa do all of the work in the house. They sat like queens, while Vasilissa scrubbed and chopped, cooked and cleaned. She was a servant in her very own home!

Every night, weary little Vasilissa would tell her troubles to the tiny doll and be comforted by her.

When Vasilissa's father left on a trip to buy goods, the cruel stepmother hatched a plan to get rid of Vasilissa.

That night, the stepmother secretly blew out the only candle the family left burning at night.

"What shall we do?" cried the stepmother. "There is no light! Vasilissa, you must go to the witch Baba Yaga and ask her for a flame!"

Vasilissa sat down and fed her doll a bit of food.

"I am frightened!" she told the doll. "I need your help!"

"Do not worry," the doll replied. "I will protect you."

Baba Yaga lived deep in the forest that bordered the village. Vasilissa stumbled through the dark woods until she came to Baba Yaga's hut. It was perched on chicken legs with animal skulls hanging from the gate. Vasilissa bravely entered the hut to face the old witch.

The witch told Vasilissa she must work for the light she was seeking. She made Vasilissa bring her lots of food from the oven and the old witch gobbled it all up. She gave Vasilissa a tiny scrap of bread, which the young girl tucked away in her pocket.

Baba Yaga told Vasilissa that the next day she would have to scrub the floors, do the washing, cook supper, and clean an entire bushel of wheat while Baba Yaga was away. Otherwise, she would never allow Vasilissa to go home ever again.

When Baba Yaga fell asleep, Vasilissa took out her doll and told her of the witch's demands.

The doll said, "Go to sleep. You have nothing to fear."

When Vasilissa awoke the next morning, Baba Yaga was gone. Vasilissa found that all of her tasks had already been done! Vasilissa thanked her doll and rested.

When Baba Yaga returned, she was astounded.

"How did you finish this work?" she demanded.

Vasilissa could not tell her about the doll, but she wished to be truthful.

She said, "My mother's blessings helped me."

The witch screamed, "Blessings! We will have no blessings in this house! Be off with you!"

Vasilissa ran as fast as she could. As she passed the fence, she grabbed a glowing skull for light.

When she reached her home, Vasilissa found that her stepmother and stepsisters had fled. They did not want her father to know what they had done to Vasilissa.

The next day, Vasilissa's father returned from his journey. When Vasilissa saw him, she wept tears of joy. Vasilissa and her father lived together happily. She kept her doll and her mother's blessings with her always.

Beauty and the Beast

Adapted by Amy Adair
Illustrated by David Merrell

There once was a rich man who had three daughters. After a lifetime of prosperity, he fell upon hard times when the ships he owned were lost at sea.

His family was forced to move into a small cottage, which made his two elder daughters very unhappy. But the man's youngest daughter, Beauty, remained hopeful.

One day, he received word that one of his lost ships had sailed safely into harbor.

He decided to make the difficult journey to port to see the ship. But when he reached the port, he learned that his ship had been robbed.

Sadly, he started on his long trip back home. It was snowy and he could barely see the trail before him. Just then, he saw a castle rising ahead of him like a happy dream!

As he made his way towards the castle he spotted green trees and a lush garden in the distance. A well-fed horse slowly drank from a gushing water fountain.

He had stumbled upon an enchanted castle! He saw a row of flowering trees and felt a summery breeze on his wind-burned face.

The man slowly approached the castle and rang the bell several times. When no one answered, he stepped inside to explore the grand castle.

He wandered around until he found a table filled with food. He helped himself and then fell into a deep sleep by the warm fire.

The next morning, as he was leaving the castle through the gardens, the man spotted a rosebush. He plucked a few roses for his daughters.

Suddenly, the man was shocked to see a giant beast block his path. The beast was very angry!

"Is this the thanks I get for helping you?" roared the huge beast. The terrified man explained that the flowers were a gift for his daughters.

The beast decided to strike a deal.

The beast demanded that the man give up one of his beloved daughters to repay the debt for taking the roses.

"Please, beast. Take me, instead!" pleaded the man.

But the beast would not change his mind. He did, however, allow the man to return home and tell his children what had happened.

The two elder daughters refused to go to the beast.

"I will go," said Beauty quietly. "You have sacrificed so much for us, Father. Please, let me help you."

Beauty and her father went to the beast's castle and she sat down at the dinner table to meet the beast.

"Are you willing to stay with me in order to save your father?" he asked

At first Beauty was frightened by his terrible face and hulking size, but he spoke gently to her.

Beauty looked into the beast's eyes and saw that they were kind. "Yes," she answered, "I will stay."

The next day, after Beauty's father left, she began trying to make the castle her home. The beast had given her a special room. It had mirrored walls and a clock that woke her by calling out her name.

Every evening she dined with the beast. Then Beauty and the beast would stroll together through the enchanted garden filled with beautiful flowers.

One day, the beast asked Beauty to marry him.

"Oh, please do not ask me that," she told the beast. "I am happy here with you, but I miss my family terribly!"

Although the beast knew he would miss Beauty, he allowed her to return home for a brief visit.

He let Beauty fill a trunk with gifts for her family and gave her a special gift — a magic ring. When she put the ring on her finger, it would take her wherever she wished and Beauty knew that it would help her see her family.

Sure enough, Beauty put the ring on her finger and found herself back home. Her family was delighted to see her and Beauty was so happy to be with them once again.

Later, as Beauty pulled gifts from the trunk, her family marveled at the beast's generosity.

"This is the most beautiful necklace I have ever seen," Beauty's eldest sister said.

Beauty's family made a wonderful feast that night to welcome her home. Everyone gathered around and listened while Beauty described the enchanted castle and the beautiful gardens.

She also told them how much she had grown to care for her friend, the beast. She said she enjoyed his company and their long talks.

As the days passed,Beauty began to miss the beast. While she was happy to be with her family, Beauty longed to walk around the grounds with her friend, the beast.

One night, Beauty took the magic ring out of her jewelry box and placed it on her finger. But, when she looked deep into the jewel, she focused her eyes on a very troubling and disturbing sight.

Beauty saw the beast lying in his garden. He looked like he was very ill. "Oh, my poor beast!" cried Beauty. With that, she turned the ring on her finger and was magically returned to the garden to help the beast.

Beauty found the beast lying on the ground and rushed to his side. When she lifted his head, he opened his eyes. He wanted to look at her one last time.

Beauty recalled how she kept thinking about the beast while she was home with her family. She knew that she must tell him how she really felt about him.

"Please don't leave me!" cried Beauty. "I love you!"

The beast's eyes lit up when he heard Beauty say those three wonderful words.

Suddenly, there was a blinding flash of light, and the monstrous beast was transformed into a handsome prince!

"Thank you!" exclaimed the prince. "Many years ago, I was placed under a spell by an evil enchantress. Only true love could have released me from it," he explained as he took Beauty's hand.

"Will you marry me, Beauty?" the prince whispered.

"Yes," answered Beauty.

Beauty and her prince lived happily ever after.

Twelve Dancing Princesses

Adapted by Michael P. Fertig
Illustrated by Jeffrey Ebbeler

Once upon a time in a faraway kingdom, there lived a king with twelve daughters. To say having twelve daughters was a handful would be unfair to the king, for it was far more than that. The king was a very protective father, and he worried about his little princesses. Also, he did not always understand their ways. This was especially true since the death of his dear and lovely wife many long and lonely years ago.

Each night, the king carefully locked the door to his daughters' bedroom. Yet, each morning, he found the princesses tired and out of sorts.

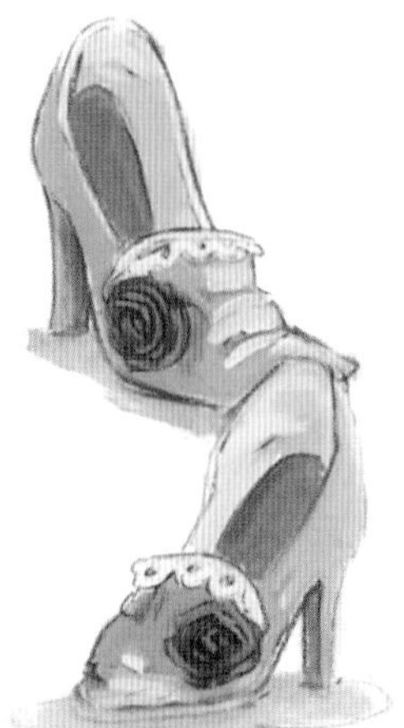

The king was even more puzzled because every morning he would find that their new pairs of silk dancing slippers had been worn to shreds.

When the king asked his daughters about this, they would laugh and say, "Don't be silly, Father. We go to sleep each night and sleep soundly until the morning."

But the king was not convinced. He decided to offer a reward to any man from his kingdom who could solve this mystery.

The next day, one of the king's subjects — a man called Rawling — was out walking in the countryside. He was a poor but clever man, and he liked to walk and think.

One day, Rawling had stopped to eat his modest lunch when a strange little woman came hobbling by.

"Good day," said Rawling, standing to greet her. "Would you care for some lunch?"

"Thank you," said the old woman. "You are very kind to share with me when you have so little." In return, she gave him a cloak that could make him invisible. "Take it to the castle," she said, "and claim the king's reward."

Thanking the old woman, Rawling set off for the castle. When he arrived, the king was eager to see if this young man would succeed in solving the mystery.

When Rawling met the princesses, they offered him a goblet of wine.

"Thank you," said Rawling. But he was suspicious that it contained a sleeping potion. When the princesses turned away, Rawling poured it beneath the table.

Rawling pretended to yawn. He was then shown to his bed, where he pretended to fall into a deep and dreamless sleep.

"It is safe now," said the eldest princess. "We have made sure he will sleep through the night."

With that, she tapped three times on a bedpost, revealing a secret staircase.

The princesses were in a flurry as they put on their best ball dresses and prepared to leave the castle.

After preparing for their escape, the twelve princesses ran down the winding stairs.

Rawling, wearing his cloak, followed. He stepped upon the youngest princess's gown. She was startled but could see no one when she turned around.

At the bottom of the stairs was an enchanted forest. The trees had branches of gold, silver and glittering diamonds.

Twelve princes met the princesses and guided them to gondolas. Then they rowed across a lake to a beautiful castle on a hill.

Wearing his invisible cloak, Rawling sneaked onto one of the boats.

The prince who was rowing one of the boats thought it seemed a lot heavier than usual!

They soon arrived at the castle and the princesses gingerly stepped off the gondolas.

The twelve princesses and the twelve princes walked arm in arm into a grand ballroom within the castle.

Rawling crept softly behind them, marveling at all that he saw in this grand and beautiful ballroom.

Lyrical music seemed to float from the ceiling. Clusters of candles hung in the air, casting a warm and magical glow.

The princesses and princes began to dance splendidly around the enchanted, candlelit ballroom.

Rawling watched, enthralled, as each pair seemed to move even more gracefully than the next couple.

The pairs danced for hours, pausing only to sip punch from goblets.

Then, finally, the princes escorted the twelve princesses back to the secret staircase in the castle.

Fortunately, the twelve princesses were tired from their evening of dancing so they walked slowly. Rawling was able to hurry ahead of them and slip back into his bed before they returned.

The youngest princess peeked in on him.

"Our handsome guest is sleeping as though he has lived a thousand lives," she told her sisters. With that, the princesses removed their tattered dancing slippers and placed them in a row. Then, they climbed into their own beds and fell asleep.

The next morning, Rawling crept out of bed to seek out the king and reveal his discoveries.

"Your Majesty," said Rawling, "I have solved your riddle. It seems that your lovely daughters wear out their slippers by dancing late into the night." And he told the king all that he knew.

The king listened intently. "Can you produce proof of this story?" he asked.

Rawling presented a gleaming golden goblet that was beautifully engraved. "This, Your Majesty, is a goblet from the castle," Rawling said. "I ask you to put your lips to it."

The king raised the goblet to his lips, and it instantly filled with punch.

"How is this possible?" asked the king.

"The goblet is enchanted," said Rawling.

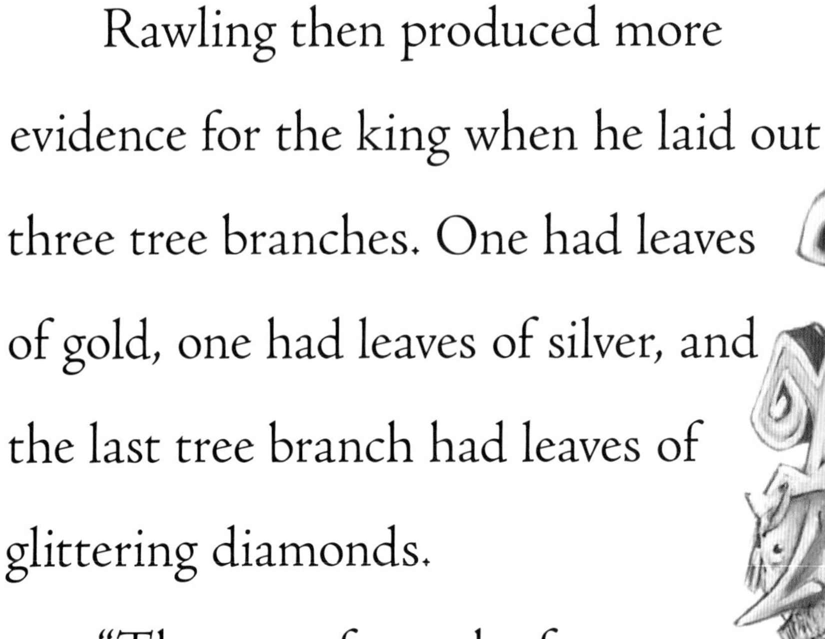

Rawling then produced more evidence for the king when he laid out three tree branches. One had leaves of gold, one had leaves of silver, and the last tree branch had leaves of glittering diamonds.

"These are from the forest near the castle," Rawling explained. "But the greatest proof of my tale must come from your own beautiful daughters."

The princesses, who were listening at the door, confirmed what he had said to their father.

The king was pleased that Rawling had solved the mystery and said to Rawling, "I owe you a great reward."

"Your Majesty," spoke Rawling, "I have grown fond of your youngest daughter, and if she will agree, I would like for her to marry me."

The princess was also quite smitten with Rawling and agreed to marry him with the king's consent.

The pair lived — and danced — happily ever after.

Snow White and the Seven Dwarves

Adapted by Lara Ehrlich
Illustrated by Barbara Lanza

Once upon a time in a peaceful kingdom by the sea, the king and queen were blessed with a baby girl. Her hair was black as night, her lips were red as rubies, and her skin was white as snow. The queen named her beautiful daughter Snow White.

All the people in the kingdom rejoiced, but their joy was short-lived, for the queen soon fell ill and died.

After many months, the king remarried. However, the woman he chose as his bride was very different from Snow White's kind and beautiful mother.

The new queen was wicked and vain. She cared for nothing but her own beauty.

Every morning, the queen would visit her magic mirror and ask the same question: "Mirror, mirror, on the wall, who is the fairest of all?"

The magic mirror always replied, "You, my queen, are the fairest of all."

For many years, the mirror always gave the queen the same answer.

The queen gave no thought to Snow White, who had grown into a very beautiful young woman.

One day, the queen visited the mirror with her usual question. This time she received a different answer.

"You, my queen, may have a beauty quite rare, but Snow White is a thousand times more lovely and fair."

Mad with jealousy, the queen sent for the royal huntsman with an evil order.

She commanded the huntsman to take Snow White into the forest and kill her at once. Fearing for his life, the huntsman took Snow White into the woods. When she looked up at him with trusting eyes, the huntsman could not bring himself to carry out the queen's order. He left Snow White in the forest and warned her never to return to the castle.

The sky grew dark as Snow White wandered deeper and deeper into the forest. She was terribly frightened, but Snow White willed herself to continue walking through the night.

Just when Snow White feared she could not take another step, she found herself in a clearing beside a tiny cottage. She knocked once on the wooden door, but there was no answer.

However, the force of her knock caused the door to swing open, and Snow White stepped inside.

She saw seven little cups and seven little plates on a table surrounded by seven little chairs. Seven little nightshirts hung on seven little hooks, and along one wall stood seven little beds. The cottage was cozy but untidy.

"Perhaps if I tidy this little cottage," she thought, "the owners won't mind if I have a bit of dinner and warm myself by the fire."

Snow White cleaned the cottage until it shone. Only then did she take a slice of bread. She sat down on one of the beds to wait for someone to come home. Snow White was so tired, and the little bed was so cozy, that she soon fell into a deep and dreamless sleep.

While she slept, seven dwarves entered their little home. They chattered away as they opened the door but fell silent at the sight of the maiden sleeping on the bed.

Snow White awoke to find herself surrounded by seven kind faces. The dwarves welcomed her to the cottage and asked how she had found their home. Snow White told the dwarves about the evil queen and her flight through the dark forest.

The dwarves took pity on Snow White and asked her to stay with them. She was happy to keep the house tidy and make delicious meals for the dwarves. Snow White felt right at home in their cottage.

Back at the castle, the evil queen gazed into her mirror and asked, "Mirror, mirror, on the wall, who in this realm is the fairest of all?"

The mirror replied, "You, my queen, have a beauty quite rare, but beyond the mountains, where the seven dwarves dwell, Snow White is thriving, and this I must tell: Within this realm she's still a thousand times more beautiful and fair."

The queen flew into a rage. She began to search for Snow White. When the queen found the cottage in the clearing, she disguised herself as a poor seamstress, calling out, "Gowns for sale!"

Snow White had finished her work for the day and was in very good spirits. She thought that it would be nice to have a pretty new dress, so she greeted the seamstress and welcomed her into the tidy little cottage that she shared with the seven dwarves.

Snow White slipped into one of the beautiful dresses and asked the seamstress to adjust the stitchings on the dress. The evil queen pulled the laces so tight that Snow White could not breathe, and she fell to the floor, bound in the lovely gown.

The dwarves came home that evening to find Snow White lying motionless on the ground. They quickly cut the laces and Snow White opened her eyes.

That night the queen triumphantly asked her mirror, "Mirror, mirror, on the wall, who is the fairest of all?" Again, the mirror replied that Snow White was the fairest in the land.

White with rage, the queen filled the teeth of her prettiest comb with deadly poison. The next morning, she disguised herself as a peddler and set out through the woods to the little cottage in the clearing.

Snow White welcomed the peddler into the cottage, never guessing that it was really the evil queen. Snow White admired all the silver combs. The queen selected the most beautiful one and gently combed Snow White's long, black hair. The moment the comb touched her head, Snow White fell to the ground, her thick tresses tangled around her.

When the dwarves returned home, they found Snow White on the floor. As the sad dwarves carried the girl to her bed, the comb fell from Snow White's hair. She opened her eyes and smiled up at them.

The dwarves were happy to see that Snow White had been revived, but they were worried that the queen would try to harm Snow White again. They made Snow White promise not to open the door for anyone but themselves.

The queen returned to the mirror and gazed proudly at her reflection. "Mirror, mirror, on the wall, who in this realm is the fairest of all?" Again, the mirror answered that Snow White was a thousand times fairer than the queen.

Shaking with fury, the queen thought for a very long time. Finally, she was certain that she had an idea that would not fail. The queen plucked the finest apple from the orchard and poisoned the shiniest half. She disguised herself as a poor farmer woman and set off through the woods, carrying a basket of apples on her arm.

"Apples for sale!" the queen called out from the yard. This time, Snow White heeded the seven dwarves and did not open the cottage door.

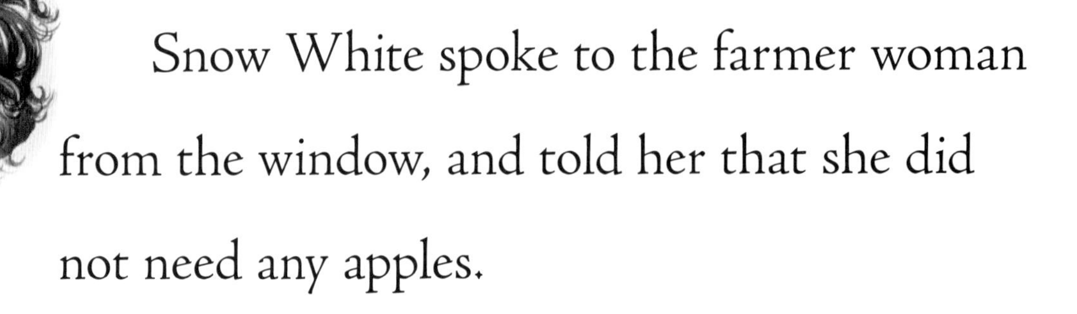

Snow White spoke to the farmer woman from the window, and told her that she did not need any apples.

The queen held the poisoned apple up to the window and said, "You must share this delicious apple with me."

The queen cut the apple in half and ate the unpoisoned half herself. She gave the poisoned half to Snow White, and the poor trusting girl took a bite and fell lifeless to the ground.

When the dwarves returned home, they knew that they could not awaken Snow White. Sadly, they placed her in a glass case.

One day, a handsome prince rode through the forest and saw the dwarves watching over Snow White.

When the prince asked the dwarves what had happened, they told him what the wicked queen had done to Snow White.

The prince said, "I will take her to my castle until she awakens. Then I hope she will agree to marry me."

As the prince moved the glass case, a bit of poisoned apple fell from Snow White's mouth. She woke up and smiled at the dashing prince!

The couple were soon married, and lived happily ever after.

The Wild Swans

Adapted by Lara Ehrlich
Illustrated by Kathy Mitchell

Once upon a time in a faraway land, there lived a good king and his four children. His wife had died, leaving him to raise three sons and a daughter on his own. The queen had been a beautiful and gentle woman who had spent her days in the garden among her rosebushes.

The king's youngest child, Rosalind, reminded him of the queen. From the time she was small, Rosalind loved to tend her mother's roses. As she grew, Rosalind was as good and kind a daughter as any man could wish for.

The king's three brave sons spent their hours as most princes do, hunting in the forest. One day, they caught sight of a white stag at the edge of the clearing.

They chased the stag through the forest from dawn until dusk, but it slipped soundlessly through the brush. As night fell, the princes followed the stag into the kingdom of Queen Maeve, the ruler of the fairies. Queen Maeve heard the princes crashing through her trees and, in a rage, turned them into wild swans.

Wailing mournfully, the swan princes flew over the castle walls and disappeared into the night sky. Rosalind heard their cries and opened her window. She saw her beloved brothers rise in front of the moon and disappear.

The king fell into a deep sadness. Even Rosalind, who had always made her father so happy, could do nothing for him. So Rosalind took leave of her father and set out in search of her brothers. She traveled far and wide, until one evening she came to an ocean. On the shore, Rosalind found three white feathers.

As she bent to gather the feathers, an old woman wandered down the shore carrying a very heavy basket. Rosalind took the old woman's basket upon her own back and helped her cross the rocky beach.

"Thank you, my dear," the old woman said, smiling kindly. "What are you doing here all alone?"

Rosalind clutched the three feathers to her breast and replied, "I am searching for my brothers who have been transformed into swans. Have you seen any swans nearby?"

The old woman nodded thoughtfully and pointed toward a rocky cove in the distance. Rosalind turned her head to look. When she turned back again, the old woman had mysteriously vanished.

Rosalind hid in the brush to wait and see if the swans would appear. Finally, as the sun began to set, three swans flew over the ocean and came to rest in the cove.

Although she longed to call out to them, Rosalind held her breath for fear that she would frighten the swans away. As the last of the sun's rays disappeared over the horizon, a startling change occurred. The swans lifted their long necks and transformed into men. Rosalind could wait no longer and ran onto the beach, into her brothers' arms.

"We have only until sunrise," the princes told her. "Then we will become swans once again, and we must fly back over the ocean."

"Then I will go with you," Rosalind replied.

The princes worked all night making a net to carry their sister. At dawn, when they again became swans, they carried her over the ocean to their cave.

While her brothers hunted for food, Rosalind curled up and dreamed of the old woman on the beach.

In Rosalind's dream, the old woman transformed into a beautiful and frightening queen.

"I am Queen Maeve," the queen told her. "Because of your kindness to me, I will give you one chance to save your brothers. But it will require great sacrifice from you."

Queen Maeve swept her arm across the cave, and rosebushes appeared all around her.

"From these roses, you must craft three shirts, one for each brother. When you cover the swans with them, the spell will be broken. But you may not speak until the shirts have been completed. If you do, your words will pierce your brothers' hearts like arrows."

Rosalind awoke to find the cave filled with rosebushes. When her brothers returned, she was sewing the rose petals into a fine cloth. Although she could not explain, her brothers knew that she was helping them.

The swan princes brought Rosalind food and water and kept her warm in the shelter of their wings. She worked for many days and nights, barely pausing to rest.

One evening, a woodcutter and his wife discovered the cave as they were walking along the shore. The woodcutter's wife had never seen such lovely roses, and she stepped inside the cave for a closer look.

There, among the roses, she found Rosalind sewing petals into cloth. The couple took pity on the young girl alone in the cave. They insisted she return with them to their cottage, and Rosalind could not speak to resist.

As they left the cave, Rosalind gathered as many roses as she could carry. She stayed with the couple for many days and did all that they asked of her. But Rosalind did not forget her dear brothers. She spent every spare moment sewing their garments from rose petals.

When two shirts were complete and the third lacked only a sleeve, Rosalind sewed the last petal from her final rose. What could she do? She had to finish her task.

The woodcutter's wife had a rosebush that she loved above all else. Rosalind wept as she crept outside into the dark and plucked the petals from the beloved flowers. She sewed through the night, and at sunrise, she had finished the last shirt for her brother.

"You have stolen my roses!" cried the woodcutter's wife when she saw what Rosalind had done.

Rosalind fled from the house with the shirts. She raced toward her brothers, calling to them as she ran. When they heard her cries, they flew down from the sky. Rosalind quickly threw the shirts over them. The instant she did so, the three swans were transformed into three handsome princes.

Now that the spell was broken, Rosalind returned to the cottage to tell her story to the woodcutter and his wife.

"I am sorry to have hurt you when you were so kind to me," she said. "My brothers and I will repay you."

When all was forgiven, Rosalind and her brothers began their long journey home.

The good king had all but given up hope of seeing his children again. When Rosalind and her brothers returned, the king was certain that his eyes deceived him. Only when his children flocked around him and swept into his arms could he believe it was true. The kingdom commenced a celebration that lasted for many months.

The princes were careful never to hunt in Queen Maeve's forest again, and Rosalind returned to her rose garden. She sent her loveliest rosebush to the woodcutter's wife, and the roses bloomed all year round.

The Frog Prince

Adapted by Michael P. Fertig
Illustrated by Kathy Mitchell

Once upon a time in a kingdom far away, there lived a king who had many beautiful children. The king's youngest daughter, Princess Annabel, was the most playful of the royal family.

Princess Annabel loved to explore the many lovely gardens that surrounded the castle. Her favorite toy was a golden ball that her father had given to her. Again and again, she would toss the ball into the air, catching it as it fell back down. It was a game she was quite good at — until the day she threw the ball too high. It bounced wildly off of a tree branch and fell into the well in the center of the garden.

Annabel ran to the edge of the well. It was much too deep for her to climb into. She began to cry softly. She loved her golden ball.

"Please, don't cry," said a little voice.

"Who's there?" asked Annabel. She looked around, but no one else was in the garden. There was only a little frog looking up at her. "You did not speak just now, did you?" she said to the frog.

"Well, of course I did," said the frog. "I hate to see princesses cry. I will swim to the bottom of the well and find your ball. But you must do something for me."

"Yes, anything," said Annabel. "Would you like for me to give you a kiss?"

"A kiss?" said the frog with a grimace. "No, thank you. All I want is for you to invite me to dinner tonight with you and your family."

"Certainly," said Princess Annabel.

The little frog dove right into the well and swam to the bottom. He easily found the golden ball and swam back to the surface with it.

"Oh, thank you," said Annabel. "Now, please join my family and me for dinner."

Annabel scooped up the frog and headed back to the castle, just as dinner was being laid on the table.

"What is this frog doing here?" asked the king.

Annabel quickly explained her agreement with the kind and helpful frog.

"Very well," said the king. "If you made a promise, then you must keep your word."

No sooner had the first serving platter been placed on the table than the frog began to eat with messy delight. The family watched in amazement as the frog slurped and drooled all over the royal tablecloth.

The little frog ate enough to feed an army of frogs. He ate bread rolls and tossed salad, honey ham and butter-browned turkey, wild potatoes, and corn chowder.

Princess Annabel was embarrassed that her dinner guest made such a mess at the table. Clearly, this little frog did not have proper manners.

"I hope you have left some room for dessert," she said. After the kindness the frog had shown her, she wanted to be sure he enjoyed his meal. "Here, little frog, you have the first piece of cake."

The frog looked up at her with wide eyes and a big smile. He ate his piece of cake in three bites.

Suddenly, a strange rumbling came from the frog's tummy. Princess Annabel and her father watched in disbelief as the little frog turned into a boy! A prince!

The king stood and looked down at the boy. He could not believe his eyes!

Annabel was in shock. She did not know what to think. "What is happening, Father?" she asked.

"I can explain," said the prince. "My name is Prince Henry. Many years ago, an evil witch cast a spell on me, making me a frog for all eternity. The only way the spell could be broken was for a princess to offer me a piece of cake from her dinner table. I never imagined it could be broken. I am forever grateful for this meal."

"But you are so young," said Annabel.

"I was your age when the spell was cast," he said. "Once I became a frog, I never aged. I look the same today as when I was cursed. But I'm afraid I have been a frog for a very long time. My family and friends are gone. Now I have nowhere to go."

The king decided to adopt Prince Henry.

"We have more than enough room for you," said the king. "And you can play catch with my daughter."

The Goose Girl

Adapted by Lisa Harkrader
Illustrated by Cindy Salans Rosenheim

Once there was a princess who was betrothed to a prince whom she had never met. He lived in a distant kingdom. When it was time for the princess to join him there, her mother, a kind and generous queen, gathered clothes and jewels and linens to supply her daughter with everything she would need in her new home.

Then the queen gave her daughter one last gift.

"This is my royal ring," said the queen. "When you arrive at your new castle, this ring will prove who you are."

The princess slipped the ring onto her finger. Then she set out on her journey with her lady-in-waiting and her beloved horse Falada, who had the gift of speech.

After the little group had traveled for some time, the princess grew thirsty, so they stopped by a stream. The princess knelt daintily on the bank and drank from her cupped hands.

As she dipped her hands into the water, her mother's ring slid from her finger. The princess did not notice, but the lady-in-waiting did. The maid waded into the stream and plucked the ring from the current.

"Dear princess," said the lady-in-waiting, "look what I found in the stream." She held out the royal ring.

"Oh, dear!" cried the princess. "You have saved me."

"Yes, I have," said the maid. "Perhaps I should keep this ring for you. And look how you've muddied your gown. You should allow me to look after your belongings. I will keep them safe for you."

"You are very good to me," said the princess. And she switched her clothes with the maid.

When the travelers reached the castle, the king and the prince were waiting.

"Show me to my room," the lady-in-waiting demanded haughtily. "I am very tired and hungry."

The king was surprised by the young lady's rudeness. But he said politely, "We are delighted that you have arrived safely, Princess."

Then he turned to the real princess, assuming that she was the servant. "We understand that you are to be our new goose girl. Welcome! We will find some room for you as well."

"Thank you," she replied. "But I am the princess."

The lady-in-waiting laughed. "You? Your clothes are mere rags." The maid extended her hand to display the queen's ring. "This ring proves that I am the princess."

The king sent the astonished princess off with the goose boy, Conrad. She did not know what to do!

Each morning, the princess and Conrad led the geese to the meadow. Each night, she slept on straw in the barn.

One day, the princess found Falada in a pasture in the farthest corner of the kingdom. He was grazing by a fence.

"Falada!" she called. "I have found you. How are you?"

"I am well," said Falada. "I am exactly where a horse should be. But you are not where a princess should be."

The princess and her beloved Falada talked for a long time. From then on, the princess insisted that she and Conrad take the geese to Falada's pasture each day. But the goose boy soon grew tired of trudging out to the far pasture every morning, and eventually he went to complain to the king.

"She talks to that horse all day," Conrad told him.

"And the horse talks to her?" asked the puzzled king.

"Yes," said Conrad. "He tells her how brokenhearted the queen would be to see her daughter tending geese."

The curious king visited the pasture himself. He saw that Conrad was right. He realized that the goose girl was the true princess!

That night, the king asked the lady-in-waiting a question. "If someone has deceived me by pretending she is a princess," he said, "should she be made to tend geese?"

The maid smiled, thinking he described the princess. "No, your majesty," she answered. "Such a girl belongs in the stable, cleaning up after the horses."

The king nodded. "That is just what you shall do."

When the king returned the royal ring to the princess, he humbly apologized. "I should have recognized a true princess by her goodness and grace, not by her fine clothes and jewels," he told her.

The princess forgave the king. She and the prince were soon married, and everyone lived happily ever after — except for the poor stable girl.

The Flying Prince

Adapted by Brian Conway
Illustrated by Kathi Ember

One day while Prince Rashar was exploring a new part of the jungle, a large parrot landed near him.

"I am the king of the parrots," it said proudly. "Hunters are not welcome in our kingdom."

"I will not harm you," promised Prince Rashar. "But tell me, how is it that you can talk?"

"Princess Saledra gave me this power so I can protect my subjects," he answered. "She is the kindest and loveliest princess in the world!"

"Then I would like to know her," said the prince.

"It is impossible," answered the parrot. "She lives far away in the city where night becomes day."

Prince Rashar decided that he must meet this Princess Saledra, so he set off to travel to her land. On his way, he came upon four arguing trolls.

"Excuse me," the prince said, "what is the trouble? Why are all of you arguing?"

"Our master left us these four magic items," the trolls answered. "But we cannot divide them fairly."

The magic items were a flying carpet, a cloth bag that produced anything wished for by its holder, a bowl that filled with water upon command, and a tool that could defeat and tie up any enemy.

"I can help you," said the clever prince. "I will shoot an arrow into the jungle. Whoever returns with the arrow shall keep all of the items."

The trolls agreed that the prince's plan was fair.

Prince Rashar shot his arrow. When the trolls began their search, the prince took the magic items for himself.

Prince Rashar sat upon the magic carpet. "Take me to the city where night becomes day," he said.

The magic carpet lifted the prince high above the jungle, and they sailed through the air. They passed over rivers and lakes and fields. After a time, the magic carpet landed near the gates of a city. Prince Rashar stopped an old woman to ask about Princess Saledra.

"Nobody sees the princess until nightfall," the woman said. "You must go to the palace and wait."

The prince hurried to the palace. When the sun set, the city was dark for a moment. Then suddenly, Princess Saledra appeared on the palace roof. Prince Rashar drew a sharp breath.

Her beauty shone more brightly than the moon. In an instant, her radiance turned night into day. The entire city was lit by the princess's glow. Then just as suddenly, she went back into the palace and night returned.

Prince Rashar was in love. He took his magic bag and said, "Give me a shawl that matches the princess's gown." A moment later, he reached in and pulled out a flowing silk shawl that matched her gown exactly.

"Carpet," he said, "take me to Princess Saledra's chamber." The flying carpet set him down gently on the palace roof. The prince crept through the window and into the princess's room.

Princess Saledra slept soundly in her bed. The prince set the shawl beside her and stopped to gaze upon her beautiful face. Then he left quietly.

The next morning, the princess awoke to find the beautiful shawl. Who had been able to match the magical silk of her dress? Princess Saledra was curious about who her secret admirer could be.

"To make such a perfect shawl," she thought, "he must have magic as strong as my own."

The next evening, Prince Rashar flew again to the princess's window. This time he knocked softly.

When Princess Saledra saw him standing on the flying carpet, she knew it was her mysterious admirer.

"Dear Princess," said the prince, bowing, "I am Prince Rashar. I have traveled far to meet you. Unlike your own great magic, mine comes from these four objects. I present them to you as tokens of my love."

The princess saw that the prince spoke from his heart. Her own heart softened when she considered the sacrifice of his gifts. The princess smiled at the prince with the brightest smile he had ever seen. The prince smiled back, reflecting her radiance.

Princess Saledra stepped gracefully onto the magic carpet. Then the two of them sailed off together, through the night that shone like day.

Thumbelina

Adapted by Brian Conway
Illustrated by Jane Maday

Once there was a woman who lived alone in a tiny cottage. She loved her home and beautiful garden but longed for a child to share her joy.

One day, an old peddler woman came to her gate.

"I believe I have something that can help you," said the peddler. She pulled out a bundle of seeds and said, "Take these and plant them in your garden. Within a month, you will find your heart's desire."

The woman thanked the peddler and planted the seeds. As soon as she watered them, a beautiful tulip sprouted from the earth.

"What a lovely flower," said the woman. She bent down to kiss its delicate petals. When she did this, the petals opened! Sitting in the center of the flower was the most beautiful child she had ever seen.

"Dear child," she said, "you are no bigger than my thumb. I shall call you Thumbelina."

The woman cared for Thumbelina like her own daughter. They spent their days in the garden, and the woman was perfectly contented at last.

One day, the woman stepped inside the cottage for a moment while Thumbelina played merrily in the garden. The tiny girl's sweet singing attracted the attention of an ugly toad who was hopping by.

"I would like to make her my wife," said the toad.

The toad snatched Thumbelina from the garden and brought her to his lily pad in a distant pond.

"Wait here while I plan our wedding," he said.

Thumbelina strained to glimpse the edge of the pond. But the water stretched as far as she could see. She knelt on the lily pad and began to cry softly.

Her tears made ripples in the pond and brought some curious fish to the surface to see what was happening above.

The fish took pity on Thumbelina because they did not like the toad one bit. They helped float her lily pad down the stream and up on a quiet shore. As she stepped on the shore, Thumbelina thanked the fish for their help.

She walked as far as her legs could carry her, but she did not know where to find her mother's garden. As night fell, she wove a tiny hammock from blades of grass.

Thumbelina searched the woods for many weeks, looking for her mother. She knew that it would soon turn cold and she did not have anywhere to stay.

One day, Thumbelina wandered farther than ever before. As night began to fall, Thumbelina found that she was a long way from her makeshift shelter.

A wolf howled in the distance, and Thumbelina began to run. In her haste, she tripped over a tree root and fell down. Suddenly, she saw a small yet sturdy door in the bottom of the giant tree trunk!

Thumbelina knocked shyly. The door opened a crack, and a little field mouse peered out. When the mouse saw the lovely girl on her doorstep, she invited her in to warm herself by the fire. After hearing of Thumbelina's plight, the kind mouse invited her to stay with her for a while.

One day, a strange sound brought the field mouse and Thumbelina to the window. There they saw a sparrow with an injured wing. He had been traveling south for the winter, but now he could no longer fly. The sparrow knew he could not survive when winter arrived.

The hospitable field mouse welcomed the sparrow into her home. Thumbelina helped him into the burrow and tried to make him comfortable.

The sparrow was surprised to see such a tiny person living with the field mouse.

"Are you a fairy princess?" he asked kind and beautiful Thumbelina.

"What is a fairy princess?" she asked.

"Someday, when my wing is better, I will show you," answered the sparrow.

"Did you sing in my mother's garden?" asked the girl.

The sparrow said that he had never sung in the garden, but his cousin had told him stories of harmonizing with a tiny girl with a beautiful voice.

Thumbelina was overjoyed. "Yes! It was I who sang with your cousin! What a glorious voice he has."

Thumbelina began to sing for the sparrow and the little field mouse. They were delighted by her sweet voice and insisted that she sing for them every day.

The days passed quickly and the leaves soon began to change. The friends all knew that they had to settle in and hunker down for the winter.

As the harsh winds of winter blew in, Thumbelina, the mouse, and the sparrow all stayed warm in the mouse's comfortable little house.

They tended to the sparrow's wing and prepared for spring.

The winter days passed quickly in the snug little burrow. The sparrow's wing soon healed, and the friends entertained themselves with stories and songs. They even made a tiny stage from a human-sized thimble!

Although she was happy, all winter long Thumbelina continued to dream of her mother and their garden. She longed to return to her mother and live in the garden once again.

When spring finally arrived, the sparrow offered to carry Thumbelina to her mother's cottage. They sadly parted ways with their friend, the kind field mouse. After they had said their farewells, the pair then flew off into the fresh spring air.

"I have a surprise for you, Thumbelina," the sparrow told her as he landed on a flower. "I have brought you to the land where the fairies live."

The sparrow then led little Thumbelina to a beautiful garden that was filled with all sorts of wonderful flowers. Thumbelina was amazed at this lush and lovely fairy garden and felt right at home.

She was happy to find such a special place!

As she looked around, a white flower opened to reveal a perfect little boy. He was just Thumbelina's size and was the prince of the fairies.

The prince asked Thumbelina to be his bride. He placed a golden crown on her head.

Thumbelina curtsied and smiled up at the prince.

"I will marry you, Prince," she answered. "But you and the fairies must come live with me in my mother's garden. I will never be happy anywhere else." The sparrow guided them over to her ecstatic mother's garden where they all lived happily ever after.

The Little Mermaid

Adapted by Natasha Reed
Illustrated by John Martinez

Deep in the ocean, a sea king lived in a castle made of coral. His kingdom was filled with colorful plants that swayed gracefully in the currents. Fish of all shapes and sizes glided between their branches, as birds do on land.

The sea king had six daughters. The youngest was the loveliest of all. She also had the most beautiful voice of all the mermaids in the kingdom.

Nothing gave the youngest princess more pleasure than to hear about the world above the sea. It seemed wonderful to her that the flowers on land had fragrance and that the fish — which were called birds there — could sing.

On her fifteenth birthday, each princess was allowed to visit the water's surface for the first time. Year after year, the little mermaid watched her older sisters take their turns. They were delighted with what they saw. But soon, since they could go up whenever they pleased, the girls lost interest.

Finally, it was the little mermaid's turn. She waved good-bye to her sisters and rose swiftly to the water's surface.

As she broke through the water, the little mermaid saw a large ship. There was music, dancing, and laughter. She swam closer and saw a handsome young prince. He was celebrating a birthday, too!

The wind began to blow harder, and the sky grew very dark. Pounding waves battered the prince's ship, and she could hear it creak and groan.

Suddenly she saw the handsome prince fall off the ship and sink into the sea.

At first the little mermaid was happy that the handsome prince would come to her father's kingdom. But then she remembered that humans could not survive beneath the sea. She decided she must take action!

She dove under the waves and used all of her strength to pull the prince's head above the water. Then she brought him safely to shore.

Tenderly, the little mermaid brushed the hair from the prince's face and gently kissed his forehead. When she heard excited shouts from the other end of the beach, she knew that she must leave the handsome prince.

She took one last look at the prince, then quickly slipped beneath the surface of the water.

For many days, the little mermaid could think of nothing but the prince. When she told her sisters, they wept with her.

"Perhaps the sea witch will agree to help you," they said.

The brave little mermaid went to the sea witch at once. When she arrived, the witch knew why she had come.

"Princess, I can give you human legs so you can walk and dance on land," she said. "But in return, you must give me your lovely voice."

The little mermaid listened and agreed to her terms.

The witch prepared the magic potion and sealed it in a bottle. Then she captured the little mermaid's voice, so the girl could neither speak nor sing.

The little mermaid swam to the surface and quickly drank the potion. She felt quite strange, and her tail began to ache. Then, before her eyes, her tail transformed into two beautiful human legs!

She found herself on a tropical beach looking out at the sea that had once been her home.

The prince was on his morning walk when he discovered the stunning, silent girl on the beach. He was mesmerized by her beauty and tried vainly to hear her voice. But she remained mum. The prince knew that he must come to the aid of this beautiful and mysterious stranger, so he took her to his palace in the hopes that he could help her gain back her voice.

The little mermaid was given fine gowns to wear. Everyone agreed that she was the most beautiful creature in the palace, but she could not talk to anyone. Instead, the girl used her graceful movements and expressive eyes to speak to those around her. She danced and glided on her new legs as though she were swimming on land.

Everyone in the palace was enchanted by the little mermaid, especially the prince. He felt as if he had met her somewhere before. As each day passed, the prince became more intrigued.

Everywhere the prince went, the little mermaid was by his side. They rode together on horseback through the sweet-scented woods. Green boughs touched their shoulders, and birds chirped around them.

She climbed with the prince to the tops of tall mountains. They wound their way higher and higher until they could see soft clouds far below them.

As the days passed, the little mermaid loved the prince more dearly. And he also grew very fond of her. She was a kind and gentle companion.

At night, when the royal household was asleep, the little mermaid would follow the broad marble steps from the palace down to the water's edge. There she would sit in the moonlight and bathe her weary feet in the cool seawater. Her thoughts would turn to her beloved family, deep in the water below.

One night, her sisters rose to the surface, singing sorrowfully as they floated on the water. She beckoned to them, and they recognized her and swam closer. They told the little mermaid how much they missed her. They pleaded with her to return with them to their land beneath the sea.

The little mermaid smiled at them. She wanted to tell them how happy she was! She could only gesture with her eyes and the graceful movements of her hands and arms. She tried to explain how wonderful it was to be with the prince.

Her sisters were comforted to see that the little mermaid was happy. After that, her sisters came to the palace every night to visit and tell her all the latest news.

Once, she even saw her father in the distance. He had not been to the surface in many years and so did not venture so near to the land as her sisters. How she yearned to speak to him!

One day, the prince and the little mermaid returned from a walk in the gardens to find the king and queen waiting to speak with the prince. They had made the acquaintance of a neighboring king, and they believed his daughter, the princess, would make a suitable bride for their beloved son.

The little mermaid felt a sudden chill. After all she had sacrificed to be with the prince, would he choose to marry another?

At the thought, her expressive eyes became brilliant with tears. Yet she smiled bravely at the prince.

The prince reached for her hand and gave her a long, loving look.

"Mother and Father," said the prince, "my true love is here. I desire no other." The prince sank to one knee and asked the mermaid to become his wife and princess of the kingdom.

Suddenly, the little mermaid's voice returned. True love had broken the spell!

Soon, the prince and the little mermaid were married. As they set sail on their wedding voyage, the king and queen waved from the shore. The little mermaid's sisters and father followed the ship out into the deep blue sea.

The little mermaid and her prince lived happily ever after.

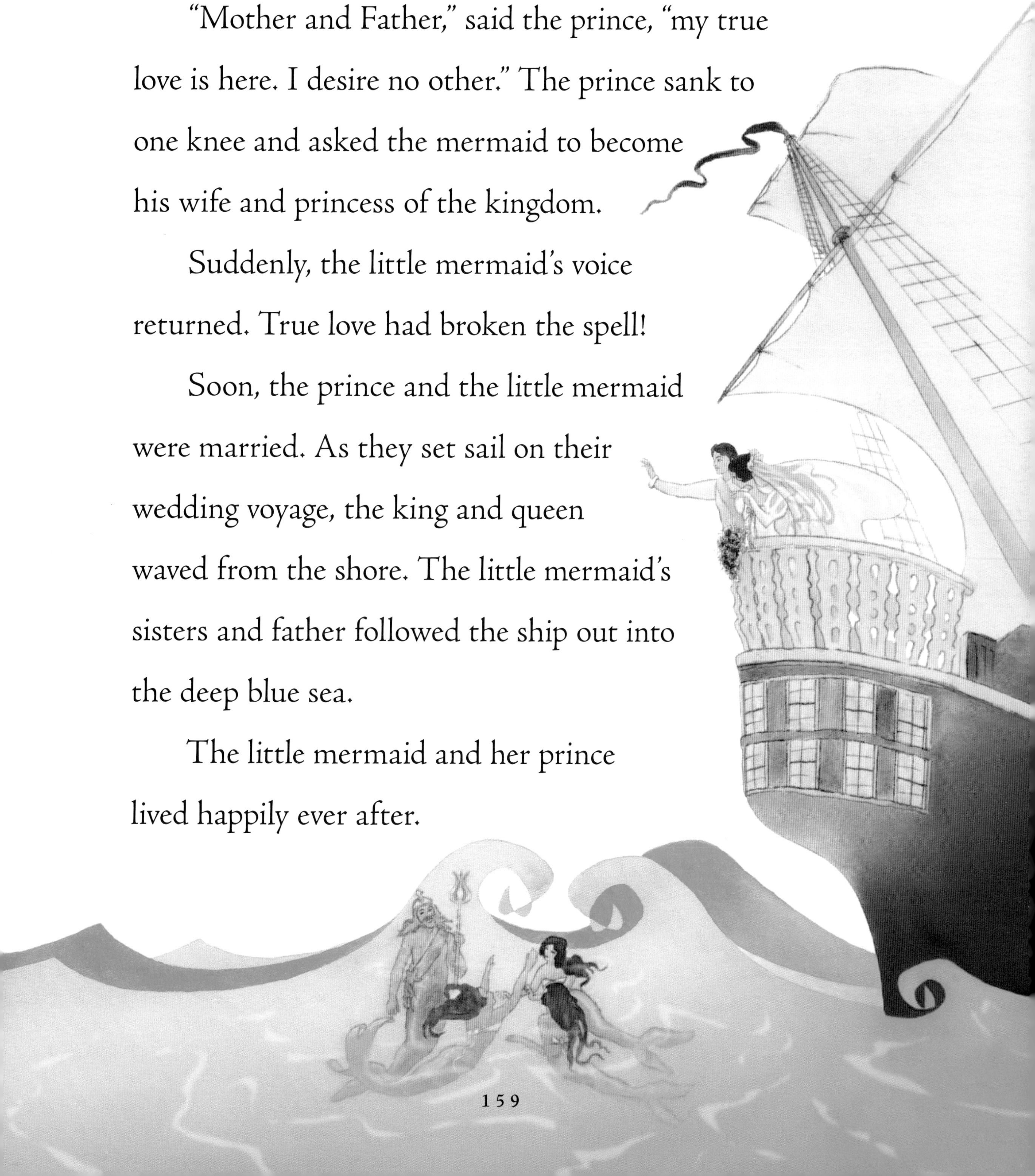

The End

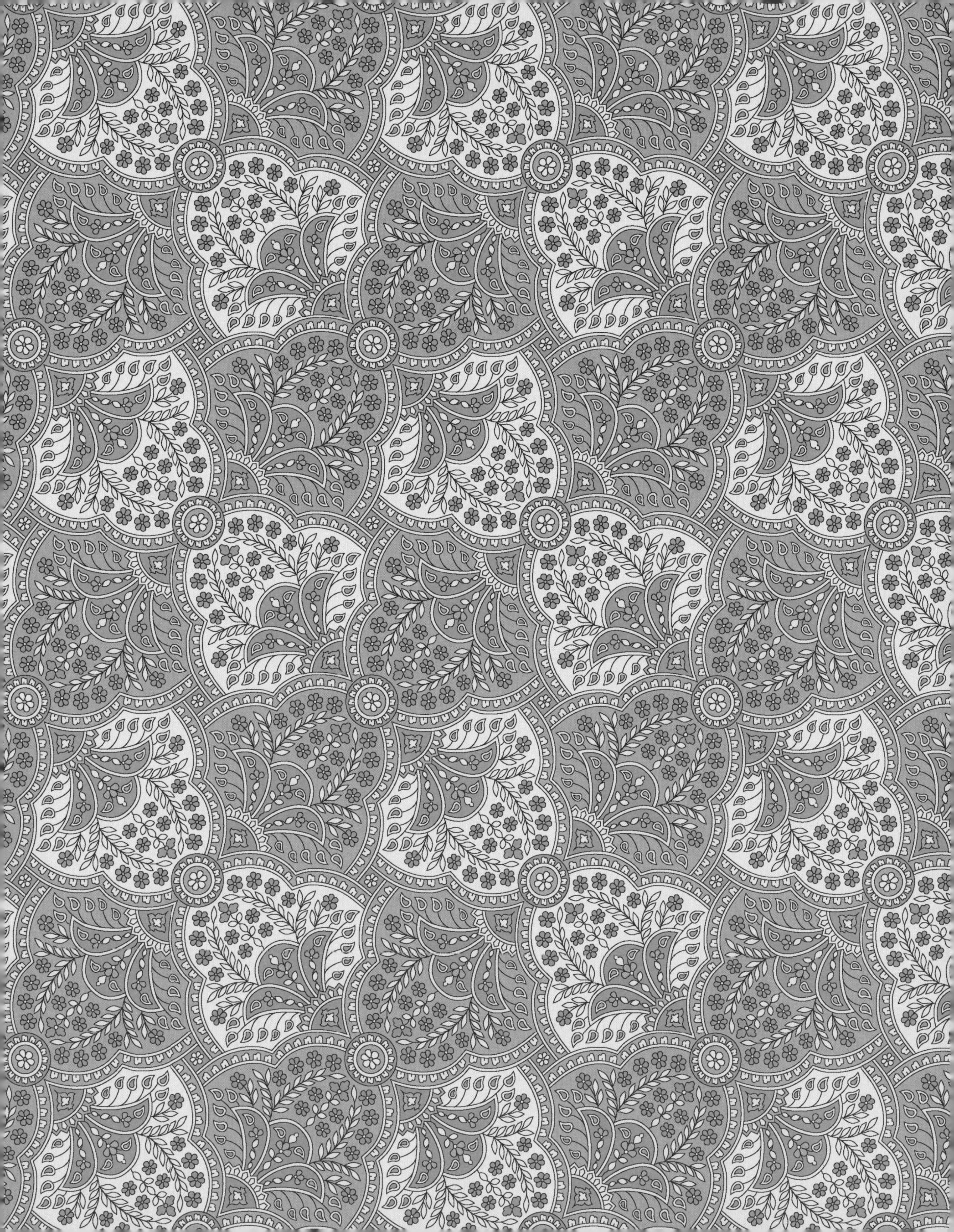

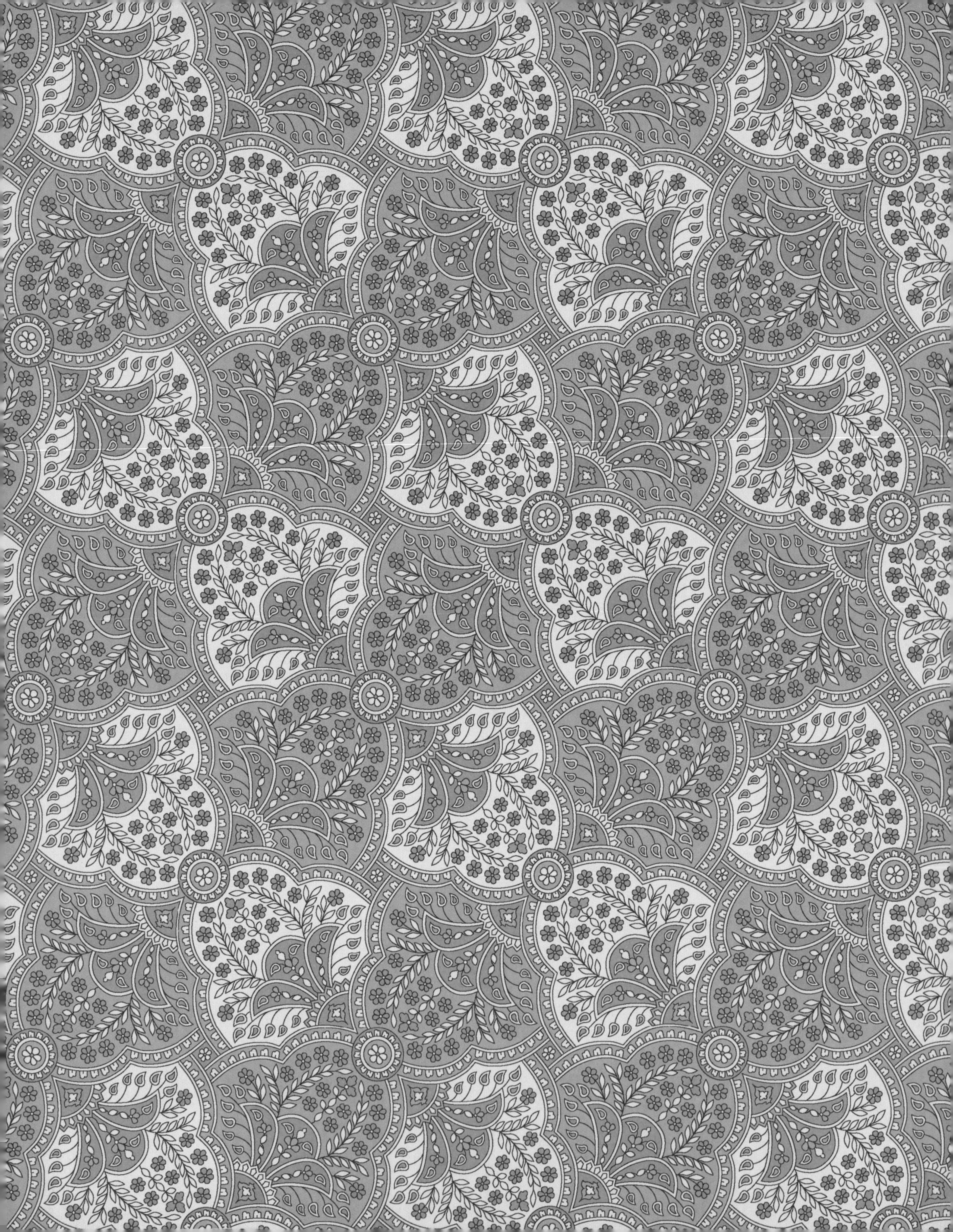